some things you should know about my dog

story and pictures by Muriel Batherman

Prentice-Hall Inc., Englewood Cliffs, N.J.

Printed in the United States of America   ·J

Prentice-Hall International, Inc., London
Prentice-Hall of Australia, Pty. Ltd., North Sydney
Prentice-Hall of Canada, Ltd., Toronto
Prentice-Hall of India Private Ltd., New Delhi
Prentice-Hall of Japan, Inc., Tokyo

10 9 8 7 6 5 4 3 2 1

Library of Congress Cataloging in Publication Data

Batherman, Muriel.
    Some things you should know about my dog.

    SUMMARY: There are a few things about
this dog that make him irresistible and unlike
any other dog.
    [1. Dogs—Fiction]   I. Title.
PZ7.B3228So   [E]   76–10172
ISBN 0–13–822544–3

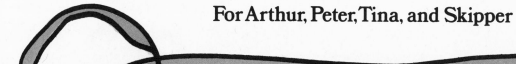

For Arthur, Peter, Tina, and Skipper

People ask me,

I tell them, "He's an extraordinary dog!"

He always follows me; he is faithful.

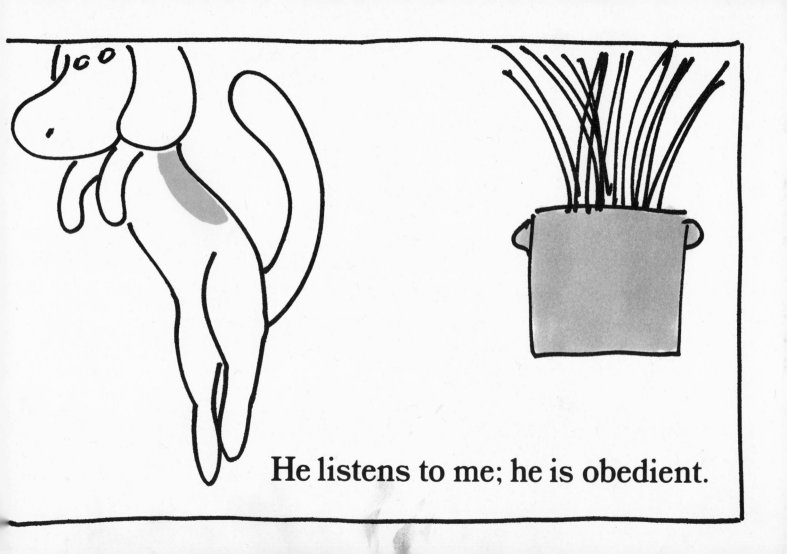

He listens to me; he is obedient.

He makes me laugh; he is comical.

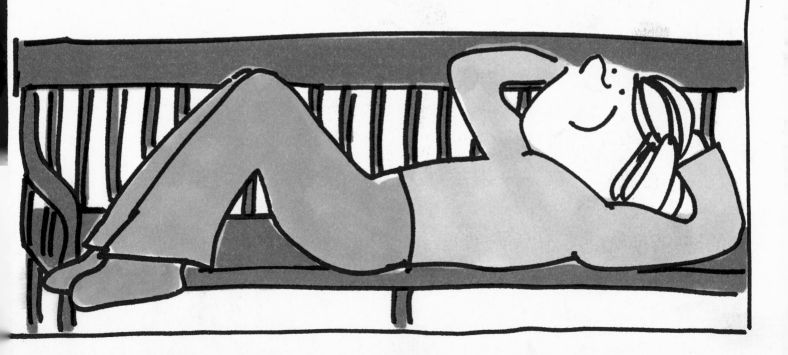

He isn't afraid of the dark; he is courageous.

He licks my face; he is affectionate.

He likes to eat with me;

he is sophisticated.

He does crazy things; he is unpredictable.

He is always sniffing;

he is curious.

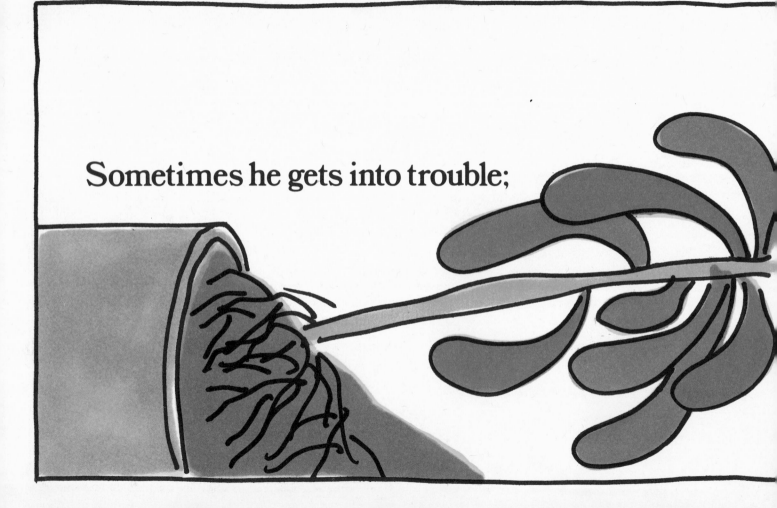

Sometimes he gets into trouble;

he is mischievous.

My dog likes to jump,

run,

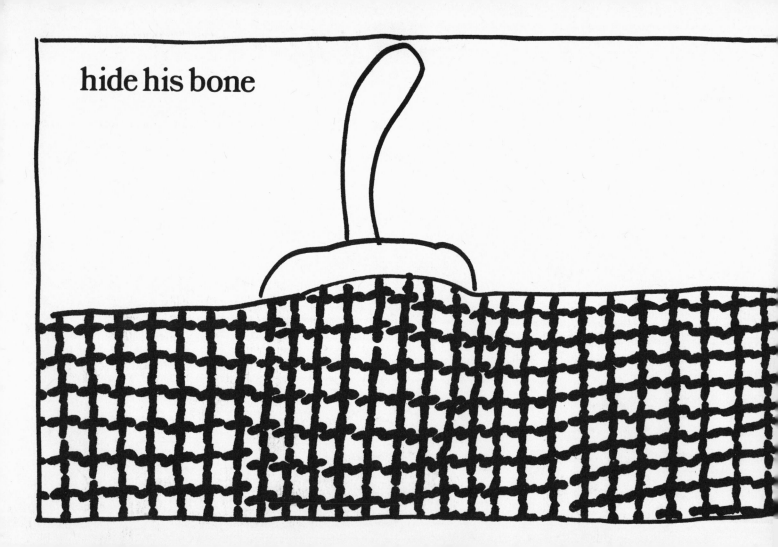

hide his bone

—and sleep.

There is no dog like my dog; he is irresistible...

I love him.